WHY SHOULD I WALK? I Can FLY!

By Ann Ingalls

Illustrated by Rebecca Evans

Dawn Publications

For my dear, darling Sadie. Fly high! —AI

For Coralin, because you know how to find the laughter in every day. —RE

Copyright © 2019 Ann Ingalls
Illustrations copyright © 2019 Rebecca Evans
Book design and computer production by Patty Arnold, Menagerie
Design & Publishing
Page 31 ornament bird and nest fonts made from oNline Web Fonts is
licensed by CC BY 3.0

Sourcebooks, Dawn Publications, and the colophon are registered trademarks
of Sourcebooks.

Published by Dawn Publications, an imprint of Sourcebooks eXplore
P.O. Box 4410, Naperville, Illinois 60567-4410 • (630) 961-3900 • sourcebookskids.com

Library of Congress Cataloging-in-Publication Data

Names: Ingalls, Ann, author. | Evans, Rebecca, illustrator.
Title: Why should I walk? I can fly! / by Ann Ingalls ; illustrated by
   Rebecca Evans.
Description: First edition. | Nevada City, CA : Dawn Publications, [2019] |
   Summary: Watercolor illustrations and simple, rhyming text follow a baby
   bird as it tries, fails, and tries again to fly.
Identifiers: LCCN 2018011985| ISBN 9781584696384 (hardback) | ISBN
   9781584696391 (pbk.)
Subjects: | CYAC: Stories in rhyme. | Birds--Fiction. | Animals,
   Infancy--Fiction. | Flight--Fiction. | Determination (Personality
   trait)--Fiction. | Perseverance (Ethics)--Fiction.
Classification: LCC PZ8.3.I56 Why 2019 | DDC [E]--dc23 LC record available at https://lccn.loc.gov/2018011985

Source of Production: Wing King Tong Paper Products Co. Ltd., Shenzhen, Guangdong Province, China
Date of Production: May 2022
Run Number: 5026787
Printed and bound in China.

WKT 10 9 8 7 6 5 4 3 2

Why should I walk? I can fly.
I've made up my mind to try.

Others can do it.
My brother's the worst.

My sister should try it.
I'll let her go first.

She did it! She flew!
And so can I.

But I'm so small,
and there's so much sky.

I hide in my nest,
not ready to budge.

And then Mother does it.
She gives me a nudge.

Flying is tricky.
Is this a mistake?

I want back in my nest,
for goodness' sake!

I grab for a branch. I grip it. Hold steady.

It slips through my feet, and I fall. I'm not ready!

Why can't I fly like those chickadees?

I beat my wings.
This flying is tough.

I rise just a bit,
then land in some stuff.

Oh no, a cat! He sees me.
Good grief!

I jump, and he misses.
What a relief!

I flap, and I flutter, again and again.

I'm tired of trying. I give up, but then...

By beating my wings for all that they're worth,
I rise up — and up — and
look down at the earth.

I zoom up and down all over the place.
I zip along with the wind in my face.

Nothing's more thrilling than winging on high.
Why should I walk? I can FLY!

Fact or Fiction?

Baby birds face many challenges when they are learning to fly—that's a fact. But some of the events in the story are exaggerated to be funny—they are fiction.

Is the bird in the story a real bird?

The bird in the story is based on a real bird—an American Robin. Robins have gray-brown backs. Their round bellies are orange. They live all across North America. You may see robins running or hopping on the grass. They're looking for worms and other small bugs to eat. They also eat berries and fruit.

Are there three babies in one nest?

Yes, a robin lays 3-4 blue eggs. The mother robin makes a cup-shaped nest out of dead grass, twigs, and mud. Nests are only used for keeping eggs warm and for raising chicks. Because nests can attract predators, parents want their young to leave the nest as soon as possible.

How old are robins when they leave the nest?

Robin eggs hatch in about two weeks. Both parents work together to feed them 100 meals a day. The babies grow quickly. They are ready to leave the nest when they are only two weeks old. Then they are called fledglings. Unlike the fledglings

shown in the story, young birds are about the same size as their parents when they leave the nest.

Does the mother push a baby out of the nest?

No, the mother does not push the babies out. As the babies get older, the mother begins to stand outside the nest to feed them. Then she moves farther and farther away. The fledglings have to leave the nest to get their food. Then they may fall or jump from a branch. They might hop and flutter from the ground back to their nest. Other times they stay on the ground.

Is it hard for baby birds to fly?

Yes and no. Birds are designed to fly. But young birds need to learn how to do it. Their muscles are weak, and they need to learn how to flap their wings. It takes practice. Sometimes they practice on the edge of the nest. If they're not strong enough, they may fall to the ground. Then they practice on the ground, like the bird in the story.

What about the cat?

It's true that a cat will catch and kill birds. Young birds on the ground are in a lot of danger. You can protect birds by keeping your cat inside, especially during springtime when baby birds are learning to fly.

What should you do if you find a baby bird on the ground?

You should leave it alone. Robins and other birds may spend some time on the ground before learning to fly. Adults will care for fledglings there. They will show them how to find food and how to stay safe. However, if a bird is hurt, call a wildlife sanctuary for advice about what to do.

Inspiration Behind the Story

by Ann Ingalls, author

I have dreamed about flying my entire life. The closest I've come is riding a zipline. I love it! I have always been intrigued by the courage it takes for a small bird to step out of the nest and venture into the larger world. All young creatures take risks, which is one of the reasons I think this story holds appeal for young children—they take risks every day. As they see one of the smaller animals on Earth try something new and fail but keep trying, I hope they'll be encouraged to keep trying, too, even though it's hard. I want to give them the message to boldly try new things and not give up.

Literacy Connection— Tips for Reading Aloud

1. Preview the book ahead of time. Plan out the pacing of the story to create a dramatic effect.

2. Show the cover, read aloud the title, and identify the author and illustrator. Ask children to predict what the book might be about.

3. Read aloud the entire text with few interruptions, pausing only to provide the meanings of unfamiliar words.

4. When finished, have children review their predictions. *What is the story about? What message did the author want to give you?* Share the author's and illustrator's messages above.

5. Read the book again. Refer to the opening illustration and ask: *Which bird is telling the story?*

6. Refer to the illustration on the next page and have student's identify the main character, mother, sister, and brother.

7. As you continue to read, ask: *What challenge is the main character facing? What is the main character feeling? What clues do you have?*

8. Read and discuss the nonfiction information about baby birds in "Explore More for Kids."

Teaching Baby Birds to Fly

by Rebecca Evans, illustrator

When I was in first grade, my mother rescued two injured baby sparrows. Once they had feathers, my sister, brother, and I taught them how to fly. Kneeling on the ground, we cupped them in our hands and gently tossed them into the air. Little by little they learned to spread their wings and fly a few feet at a time. When they could fly across the yard, we knew they were ready to leave us. On a warm summer day, we released them in a cherry orchard amidst a flock of other sparrows and said our tearful goodbyes.

Fostering a Growth Mindset

A growth mindset means acting on the belief that abilities can be developed through dedication and hard work. The little bird in the story exemplifies having a growth mindset because he kept trying new strategies until he learned to fly—he jumped, flapped, fluttered, and beat his wings. Flying was hard to do, and sometimes he felt discouraged; but he continued to put out the effort to succeed.

Help your students make the connection between the little bird and themselves. Ask children what new things they have learned to do, either in or out of school—from jumping rope to subtracting numbers. Engage children in a discussion with some of the following questions: *Did you succeed or fail the first time you tried? What did you do? What might you have done? What might you do next time?* Use "The first time I tried…" as a writing prompt or as the subject of a drawing.

STEM Activities

SCIENCE — What Makes a Bird a Bird?

Post photos of three common birds in your area. Have children work in small groups to make a list of the similar physical features they notice among the three birds. Pass out the "Bird Diagram Handout," available as a free download at dawnpub.com/activities/walk. Discuss and label the parts: feathers, wings, bill or beak, legs, feet, and tail. Explain and discuss the structures that help birds fly, including:

- Strong light skeletons with hollow bones—reduce weight

- Powerful chest muscles—for flapping their wings and soaring

- Wings that are curved on top and flatter beneath—air travels faster over the top of their wings and produces "lift"

- Tails—for balance and maneuvering

- Legs—often help with takeoff

TECHNOLOGY — Take a Peek

Nest cams are a wonderful way to view eggs hatching, baby birds being fed, and fledglings stretching their wings for their first flight. Chicks grow quickly. Choose a webcam to visit for a few minutes several times a week. Audubon (http://www.audubon.org/birdcams) and Cornell Lab (http://cams.allaboutbirds.org/) have a variety of webcams of puffins, osprey, falcons, owls, and other birds.

ENGINEERING — Which Nest is Best?

Birds are excellent engineers! Birds come in all shapes and sizes, and so do their nests. Some birds build their nests on tree branches, while others hang their nests below branches, hide their nests in bushes, make burrows in the ground, excavate holes in trees, or create depressions in sand or rocks. Give children an engineering design challenge to build a safe, warm nest. You may supply a variety of materials, or children may gather materials outside, including grass, leaves, twigs, and even soil to make mud. Some birds incorporate string, dog hair, or spider webs into their nests. When finished, have students test their nests' ability to hold "eggs" by putting three rocks into their nests. Based on the results of the test, they may want to modify their nests.

MATH — Bird by Bird

Use the story as a springboard to connect nature observation with math. Have children count the birds they see on their way home from school or on the school grounds. Do a variety of math calculations using their data, such as the following: add up the total number of birds seen, determine the maximum and minimum number of birds seen, create a bar graph showing the number of birds seen (x-axis) by the number of students who saw that number (y-axis), or count birds over several days and compare the totals.

Resources

- **National Audubon Society**—Information and inspiring bird stories (www.audubon.org).

- **Cornell Lab of Ornithology**—Bird information (www.allaboutbirds.org), citizen science projects (http://birds.cornell.edu/), elementary classroom kits (www.birdsleuth.org) and lessons (http://www.birds.cornell.edu/physics/lessons/elementary).

Scan this code to go directly to activities, lesson plans, and resources for this book, or go to **www.dawnpub.com** and click on "Activities" for this and other Dawn books.

Ann Ingalls passes the day exaggerating (writing fiction) or telling the truth (writing nonfiction). When given the choice between educating children or entertaining them with her writing, Ann chooses to do both! Ann has written nearly thirty other books for young readers. Before she was a children's writer, Ann taught elementary and special education classes and worked as a parent educator. In the classroom, Ann's students enjoyed rabbits, hamsters, gerbils, canaries, salamanders, fire belly toads, and what seemed like millions of fish. Ann lives in Kansas City, Missouri, with her husband, Winston. Please visit her at anningalls.com.

Rebecca Evans started drawing as soon as she could hold a crayon and just never stopped. She received her BA in Visual Art from Messiah College and also completed coursework from the Tyler School of Art. After working for nine years as an artist and designer, she returned to her first love—children's book illustration. She's authored and/or illustrated eighteen books. She also teaches art at the Chesapeake Center for Creative Art and is a regional Illustrator Coordinator for SCBWI. Rebecca currently lives in Maryland and enjoys spending time with her husband and four young children, while working from her home studio during every spare moment. Find her at rebeccaevans.net.

More Delightful Nature Books from Dawn Publications

Paddle Perch Climb: Bird Feet Are Neat—Meet the feet that help birds eat—so many different shapes, sizes, and ways to use them!

Noisy Bird Sing-Along—Every kind of bird has its very own kind of sound. You can tell who they are without even opening your eyes.

Daytime Nighttime, All Through the Year—Delightful rhymes depict two animals for each month, one active during the day and one busy at night.

The BLUES Go Birding series—Follow five intrepid little blue birds as they discover a remarkable variety of birds all across America and around the world.

Tall Tall Tree—Discover animals that make their home in a magnificent redwood.

Baby on Board: How Animals Carry Their Young—Tucked in pouches, gripped in teeth, propped on backs, or underneath—these are just some of the clever ways animals carry their babies.

What Others Are Saying...

Children (and parents!) experiencing the many firsts of growing up will relate to this lively story of a young robin learning to fly. The playful rhyming text and winsome watercolor illustrations give readers a bird's-eye view of the baby bird's emotions and adventures on its way to solo flight. — Sue Lowell Gallion, Children's book author, *Pug Meets Pig* and *Pug & Pig: Trick or Treat*

Hang in there, little robin! We all know what it feels like to fail, especially when we're striving to accomplish a new skill. But if it's something you really want to do, it's worth the effort. — Rudy Darling, President, Sierra Foothills Audubon Society

Dawn Publications is dedicated to inspiring in children a deeper understanding and appreciation for all life on Earth. You can browse through our titles, download resources for teachers, and order at www.dawnpub.com or call 800-545-7475.